A Campfire Story

Text: Corinne Delporte
Illustrations: Nelvana Ltd

CRACKBOOM!

Ranger Rob is looking forward to Campfire Story Night at Big Sky Park.

"Mom! Dad! Can I tell the campfire story tonight?"

"Sure," answers Dad. "And remember, the best stories are the real adventures you've had."

Rob has an idea. He is going to have a new adventure and tell everyone all about it at Campfire Story Night.

Ranger Rob puts on his ranger outfit.

RANGER HAT

BANDOLIER KIT

ROB is ranger ready to get outside

He speeds over the forest on a zipline.

Then he calls
CHIPPER, his high-tech
all-terrain vehicle, and jumps in.

He is quickly joined by his
best friend **STOMPER**
the yeti.

Hey, hey, where are we going today?

To the forest!

says Ranger Rob, as they soar high in the sky.

Rob and Stomper are talking about possible new adventures when they hear a strange noise. A park visitor is stuck in a ball. "It's Rip. It looks like he ran off the Wild Woods Roll-Around Ride," says Rob.

HeeelP!

The ball is out of control. It rolls faster and faster. Ranger Rob needs to act quickly.

Ranger kit: suction-cup fishing rod!

Rob targets the ball with his fishing rod. Once th
suction cup is attached to the ball, Rob stops it.

"Are you okay, Rip?" asks Stomper.

"I think so," he answers. "Just feeling a little dizzy."

Rip can't walk straight. He falls on the ball and it starts to roll away.

"Oh no! Hurry up, Stomper, we need to stop the ball," Rob says, as he dashes after it.

"The ball is heading toward the waterfall!" exclaims Stomper. Rob and Stomper chase after the ball. It rolls to the river and gets stuck in a tree trunk. Rob uses a big branch to free it.

"I'm almost done," says Rob, concentrating hard. Stomper wants to help, but he falls on Rob, catapulting the ball into the air.

Oh, no!

Rob uses his ranger binoculars to follow the ball.

"It's heading toward the desert. We'll never have time for a new adventure if we go there. But a good ranger doesn't give up in the middle of a mission."

Chipper, come in, Chipper.

Rob and Stomper almost catch the ball, but it bounces on a hammock and flies high in the sky toward the Frosty Fields. With his binoculars, Rob can see that it is stuck between the icebergs.

Let's go, Stomper! we need
to get there quickly,
says Rob.

Things are getting complicated.

"Rob, what can we do?" asks Stomper. "The ball is stuck."

"We'll try to push it from underwater. Chipper, diving mode!"

The icebergs are very impressive when you see them from below.

Chipper quickly finds the ball and throws it out of the water. But it lands on the monorail!

"Rob, there isn't enough time. We're going to be late for campfire night," says Stomper.

"We'll make it if we hurry!" says Rob. "Chipper, follow the monorail!"

The ball suddenly comes off the monorail and starts its crazy race in the jungle all over again.

Rob follows it, guided by Stomper, who swings on the vines up to the Jungle Restaurant. The ball bounces against the restaurant, jostling everybody inside.

Rob catches a birthday cake falling from the restaurant.
Yum-Yum, one of the park's baby elephants, sees it and decides she wants
to eat it. Rob runs away from her and chases the ball again. He is followed
by Stomper, Yum-Yum and the little boy who wants his cake back.

Rob looks at the elephant, "Sorry, Yum-Yum. It's not your birthday and it's not your cake."
Rob tries to jump on the ball to stop it but it bounces and bounces . . .

Oh, no!

. . . up to Ranger Station, surprising Mom, Dad and all the visitors there. He is soon joined by Stomper, Yum-Yum and the little boy.

"Wow, that was some entrance!" says Mom.

"So, Rob, are you ranger ready for campfire night?" asks Dad.
"No, I don't have anything to tell because I've been chasing the ball all over Big Sky Park," says Rob. "I didn't have time for a new adventure." Ranger Rob is disappointed.

"Hey, how come Yum-Yum is here with you guys?" Sam asks.
"And how did you get up here on
the ball? Tell us!" adds Dakota.
Rob and Stomper look at each
other and smile. They do
have an amazing
story to tell!

When it gets dark, Rob sits down close to the fire.
"You know what I always say: nothing like a day at Big Sky Park!
Today, my friend Stomper and I had an extraordinary adventure when
we least expected it!"

As Rob tells about their crazy day in Big Sky Park, everybody listens carefully and giggles.

The Best stories truly are our real-life adventures.

CrackBoom! Books is an imprint of Chouette Publishing (1987) Inc.

Text: adaptation by Corinne Delporte of the animated series Ranger Rob, produced by Nelvana
Limited/Ranger Rob UK Limited.
All rights reserved.
Original script written by Louise Moon
Original episode #113: A Ranger Campfire Story
Illustrations: Nelvana Ltd

 Ranger Rob is a trademark of Nelvana Limited. All Rights Reserved.

Chouette Publishing would like to thank the Government of Canada and SODEC
for their financial support.

Bibliothèque et Archives nationales du Québec and Library and Archives
Canada cataloguing in publication

Delporte, Corinne

[Histoire de feu de camp. English]
A campfire story/adaptation, Corinne Delporte; illustrations, Nelvana Ltd.
(Ranger Rob)
Translation of: Histoire de feu de camp.

Target audience: For children aged 3 and up.

ISBN 978-2-924786-43-7 (softcover)

I. Nelvana (Firm), illustrator. II. Title. III. Title: Histoire de feu de camp.
English.

PZ7.1.D44Ca 2018   j843'.92   C2017-942602-8

Printed in Canada
10 9 8 7 6 5 4 3 2 1 CHO2029 MAR2018